San Francisco Adventure

Penn Mullin

High Noon Books
Novato, California

San Francisco Adventure

Penn Mullin
AR B.L.: 3.2
Points: 1.0   UG

Cover Design and Interior Illustrations: Damon Rarey

International Standard Book Number: 0-87879-963-X

10 09 08 07 06 05 04 03
5 4 3 2 1 0 9 8 7

Contents

All aboard! Juan; Mike, their van driver; Justin; Miss Lake, their teacher; Amy; and Lisa smile for the camera before taking off on their trip.

When Miss Lake's seventh grade class entered the President's *See America the Beautiful* contest, they didn't think they had a chance to win. It was fun thinking they might, so everyone wrote and sent in a short essay on "What Do You Like Best About Being an American?"

They could hardly believe it when the letter came. It said: "The essays sent in by four members of your class were outstanding. These students have won a three-week trip across the United States with their teacher. All expenses will be paid."

The class clapped when Miss Lake finished reading the letter and Lisa, Amy, Justin, and Juan went home to pack their bags.

CHAPTER 1

A Cable Car House

"Your aunt lives in a cable car?" Juan asked Amy.

"Yes. It was made into a house after the 1906 Earthquake. The fire burned so many buildings. Many San Francisco people didn't have anywhere to live," Amy said. "So people made cable cars into houses."

"Your aunt's house must be really small," Justin said.

"Oh, it has been added onto," Amy told

him. "You'll see when we get there."

"We're almost there," Mike their van driver said.

"See if you can tell which house it is," said Miss Lake, their teacher. "Which one looks like it was made from a cable car?"

The kids all looked out the van windows. Most of the houses were alike. They were painted light colors. They were small and low in straight rows, all touching each other on both sides.

"None of these houses was ever a cable car!" Lisa said.

"Wait! Look at that one!" Justin pointed to a brown wooden house that stood all alone.

"I think there's a tiny extra roof up on top. It looks like the top of a cable car. It has little windows on the side. I bet that's the house!"

"You're right! That's Aunt Lin's house," Amy said.

"Good eyes, Justin," said Mike. "I never saw that extra roof up there." He parked the van in front of the house.

"There's Aunt Lin now!" Amy cried.

A pretty dark-haired lady hurried up to the van. Amy jumped down and hugged her aunt.

"You sure have grown," said Aunt Lin. "Your last visit to San Francisco was a long time ago."

Amy told Aunt Lin everyone's name. Then they all started up to the house.

"We are so excited about your cable car house," Miss Lake said. "Can you tell us a little about it?"

"This house belonged to my grandmother. That was Amy's great-grandmother. Her family moved into the cable car after the earthquake. Most of Chinatown had burned down so they needed a place to live," Aunt Lin said.

"So the house grew around the cable car?" Miss Lake asked.

"Yes. It slowly got bigger and bigger. Come on in. You can see for yourself." Aunt

Lin opened the door to her house.

"Wow! Here's the cable car!" Justin cried. "Right in the middle of the house!"

"Go ahead and get in it," said Aunt Lin.

The kids all climbed up the steps into the cable car. There were smooth wooden benches and windows all along the sides.

"This is so neat!" Lisa leaned out the window and waved to Miss Lake.

"Hey, what is this big thing back here?" Juan asked. He pointed to the large metal rod sticking out of the floor.

"That's one of the brakes," Aunt Lin said.

Mike jumped up into the front of the cable car. "And look here! The driver would use this lever to grab the cable in the street. Then the cable would pull the car up the steep hills."

"Sounds sort of scary," Lisa said. "What if he let go of the cable by mistake? That would be one fast trip down the hill!"

"Before cable cars, horses pulled the cars up the steep hills," Aunt Lin said. "Once a man saw the horses slip at the top of a hill. He watched the animals and car slide all the way back down."

"That's really awful," Amy said.

"Well, then the man got a smart idea. He decided to make something to pull the cars up the hills. This was a steel cable that runs under the street," Aunt Lin said. "Cable cars hooked onto it and got pulled up and down."

"What a great idea!" Mike said. "And it's still being used today."

"When can we ride a cable car?" Amy asked Mike.

"Later today. On our way down to Fisherman's Wharf," Mike said.

Lisa leaned out of another window in the cable car. "So people really lived inside this once?" she asked Aunt Lin.

"Yes. They sure did. They took out the seats so they could have some room," Aunt Lin said. "Later the seats were put back in. I read about this in my grandmother's diary."

"Did her diary tell about the earthquake?"

Amy asked her aunt.

"Yes. It has lots about that. Your great-grandmother Mai was just a young girl when the earthquake happened," Aunt Lin said.

"Did you find the diary here in the house?" Miss Lake asked.

"Yes, hidden at the bottom of an old trunk," Aunt Lin said.

"Can we see the diary?" Amy asked.

"Sure. I'd love for you to see it. But we must handle it very carefully. It is very old," Aunt Lin said. "I'll go get it."

She was back in a moment with a small brown leather book. The kids got off the cable car and gathered around her. Miss Lake and

Mike moved in close, too.

"Will you read us a little of it?" Amy asked.

"Yes, I'll read you a few of my favorite parts," said Aunt Lin. "Mai wrote in her diary on the day of the earthquake. She was living in Chinatown then." She slowly opened the old diary. The pages were very thin and brown at the edges. Aunt Lin held the book up.

"It's written in Chinese!" Amy said. The pages were covered with neat black markings that stood for words.

Aunt Lin began to read. *April 18, 1906. Today I was sure the end of my life had come.*

CHAPTER 2

The Diary

Aunt Lin read on from the diary. *I woke up this morning when Mother grabbed me from my bed. Everything was shaking. I heard screams. I had just time to snatch up my diary before we ran out into the street. People were running fast. There was smoke. Mother pulled me away from our house. Just then the bricks from our house fell into the street. Then we saw our roof fall in. Mother and I started to run. We wanted to get out of the street. We ran to*

California Street and then up the hill. We looked back at the city. It was all on fire. I thought it was the end of the world.

"The diary must be really valuable," Justin said.

"It is. Not many people know about it," Aunt Lin said. "I only bring it out for special friends." She smiled at the kids.

"What time did the earthquake hit?" Juan asked Aunt Lin.

"At 5:13 in the morning," Aunt Lin said. "San Francisco was just beginning to wake up. But many people never made it out of their homes."

"How many people died?" Lisa asked.

11

"There were about 500 people dead or missing. And 25,000 were left homeless," said Aunt Lin.

"Why couldn't they put the fires out?" Justin wanted to know.

"There were too many fires. The earthquake broke open so many gas lines. Fires started everywhere. Water lines were also broken. Then there was no way to get water to fight the fires," Aunt Lin explained.

"Didn't the fire burn for three days?" Mike asked.

"Yes, it did. And it left the city in ashes," said Aunt Lin.

"I want to hear what happened to my

great-grandmother Mai and her mother," Amy said.

"Well, I'll read you some more from her diary." Aunt Lin looked at the page again. *Mother and I kept walking up the hill. Then we saw my friend Lu Yep and his father. They gave us some water. We heard wagons were taking people to Golden Gate Park. So we got into one. It took us all day to get here to the park. Many tents are set up here. Tonight we are in one of them with ten other people. We got a hot dinner at a campfire.*

"When did Mai get back to Chinatown?" Lisa asked.

"She never went back," said Aunt Lin.

"She lived in a tent in the park for a couple of months. Remember, most of Chinatown had burned up. Mai and her mother had lost everything they owned. But one day they had some good luck. They saw this cable car standing empty on the street. It had been pulled out here by horses. No one knew who owned it. So finally Mai and her mother moved into it. And here it is today!"

"What a wonderful story," Miss Lake said. "See, kids, it's a great idea to keep a diary. Who knows? Maybe someday people will read what you wrote about our trip! You *are* all writing in your diaries every night, aren't you?"

Everybody groaned at once.

CHAPTER 3

Off to Chinatown!

"We're off to Fisherman's Wharf," Mike told Aunt Lin. "We'll drive through Golden Gate Park on the way. And we want the kids to see Chinatown, too. Especially after hearing Mai's diary."

"I'm so glad you came to see me in my funny house," laughed Aunt Lin. "I liked reading the diary to you. Now maybe you feel a little closer to San Francisco. And maybe you'll come back."

"I hope we'll all be back," Miss Lake told her. "It was great meeting you. Thank you for letting us visit your home."

"Have a grand day in the city. No fog today. You're lucky," Aunt Lin called out as everyone got in the van. They all waved to her as they headed off for Golden Gate Park.

Soon they were driving through beautiful green forests. There were lakes, meadows, rose gardens, and waterfalls all around them.

"And this is in the *city*?" Juan said.

"That's right. But can you believe this once was all sand dunes?" Mike said. "The city decided to plant all these trees and flowers. A lot of people thought nothing would grow out here. But look around you!"

"We'll come back here tomorrow," Miss Lake said. "There's so much to see—the Japanese Tea Garden, the Aquarium, the art museum. And we can rent boats on Stow Lake."

"We never have enough time to do everything!" said Lisa.

"That will make you come back," Mike told her. "Our next stop is downtown San Francisco. Anybody ready for a cable car ride?"

Everybody cheered. Mike drove towards Union Square, the center of the city. Then he parked the van. Everybody got out to wait for

Cable Car on One of San Francisco's Many Hills

the cable car.

"I hear it coming!" Juan yelled. The cable car came slowly up the street towards them.

They all climbed aboard when it stopped. Everybody wanted to be outside. The kids stood up on the sideboard and held onto the poles. Miss Lake and Mike sat on the wooden benches.

"Watch the gripman here in front," Mike said. "He uses that lever to grab the moving cable down in the street."

The car jerked forward. The gripman grabbed the cable and clanged the bell.

"Here we go!" Justin yelled.

"What makes the cable move?" Lisa asked.

"There are big powerful wheels in the Cable Car Barn near here. These wheels turn the cables for the whole city. Maybe we can go see them tomorrow," Mike said.

The cable car slowly climbed the hill ahead. The conductor collected fares.

"Let's get off at this next corner," Mike said. "We're at Chinatown!"

They jumped down from the cable car.

"Come on," Miss Lake said. "Follow me. We must enter Chinatown the right way— through the dragon gate!"

They all followed her down Bush Street. Then they saw a high gate with three arches.

"I feel like I'm in China!" Lisa said.

The gate was guarded by two stone dragons with open jaws.

"Don't worry," Miss Lake laughed. "The dragons are just welcoming you to Chinatown!"

They all went through the gate and up into the busy street ahead.

"It's like being in China!" Juan said. "Look at all the houses with the red and green roofs."

"And look at the street lights," Miss Lake said. "They're like Chinese lanterns."

The tiny street was filled with shoppers. A lot of the people were Chinese. Many wore dark jackets and baggy pants.

"Many Chinese people still like to dress in

the old way here," Miss Lake told the kids.

"Why are there so many Chinese people in San Francisco?" Juan asked.

"I can answer that. Many came in 1849. That was when gold was discovered near San Francisco," said Amy. "The Chinese came to join the hunt. My ancestors were in that group. But most Chinese people never found much gold. They couldn't pay for their boat trip back to China. So they decided to stay here and start their own businesses. And I'm glad they did," Amy said. "Or else maybe I wouldn't be here."

"I'm glad, too." Justin grinned at her.

CHAPTER 4

The Steep Way Down

Mike looked at his watch. "Our boat ride on the bay starts in thirty minutes. We'd better look for a cable car!"

"Is this the steep ride?" Justin asked.

"Yes. You'll love it," Mike told him. "Talk about straight down!"

They walked up a very steep hill to catch the cable car.

"This is the same hill Mai and her mother walked up," Miss Lake said.

"I hear the cable car coming! Let's grab this one," Mike yelled. They all ran and jumped on.

"Hold on!" cried Miss Lake as they started down Powell Street. The car seemed to move much faster downhill. The breeze felt great in their faces as the kids held tightly to the outside poles.

"Here comes your curve, Justin!" Mike yelled.

The car swung quickly around the corner. The kids hung on to the poles with one hand.

"Far out!" Juan yelled. "That was great!"

Soon they were starting down the Hyde Street hill.

"Help! This is really steep!" cried Lisa. "I hope they hold on tight to the cable!"

"Don't worry," Mike told her. "There are three different brakes on a cable car!"

The car moved slowly down the hill. Below they could see the blue water of the bay sparkling in the sun. The huge red Golden Gate Bridge spread over the entrance to the bay.

"This is the end of the line," Miss Lake said. "We are now at Ghiradelli Square."

The cable car stopped across from a big red brick building. "This used to be an old chocolate factory. Now it is full of great shops," Mike said. "And great chocolate. I know!"

Ferry at Colorful Fisherman's Wharf

"We better save it until after the boat trip," Miss Lake laughed. "Once you kids see Ghiradelli Square I bet you will not want to leave!"

"O.K. Follow me to Fisherman's Wharf," Mike said. "That's where we will catch the boat."

They walked along the edge of the bay. Many small fishing boats were tied up at docks. Crowds of people filled the sidewalks.

"The fish is *really* fresh here," Mike said. "These boats bring it in early in the morning. Then you can have it for lunch right here!"

"Speaking of lunch," Justin said. "I'm really getting hungry!"

"We'll get lunch on the boat," said Mike. He pointed to a group of red and white boats at the dock. "Let's get in line!"

They all joined the people waiting to get on the boat.

"We're lucky it's a clear day. No fog," Miss Lake said. "Sometimes the bay is so foggy you can't see anything."

"That would be scary," Lisa said.

A group of kids in wheelchairs were lining up for the boat, too. Some of them pushed their own wheelchairs with their hands. Others were pushed by adults.

A ramp was being put down from the boat. The disabled kids were boarding first.

"They sure look excited," Amy said. "That's great they'll be on the trip with us."

Then they all went aboard and started exploring the boat. There were seats and a snack bar downstairs. Everybody got hot dogs and then headed up to the top deck.

Suddenly a loud horn blared. The boat was leaving! It slowly backed away from the dock. A loudspeaker welcomed everybody. Then the boat headed towards the Bay Bridge.

"Ahead you see the world's longest bridge over open water," said the loudspeaker. "It connects the cities of Oakland and San Francisco. It is 8 miles long, 48 feet high."

The boat sailed under the huge bridge and

Creepy Alcatraz Island

then turned around. "Now you can get a good look at the port of San Francisco," Mike said. "And there is the Ferry Building tower that survived the 1906 Earthquake."

"It's getting windy up here," Miss Lake said. "And I think the fog's coming in."

"I can't believe it. The sky was all clear just a little while ago," Lisa said.

The boat started heading towards an island out in the bay.

"Now we're coming up on Alcatraz. This was the famous prison that held many dangerous criminals. Only three prisoners are known to have ever escaped from here. Now this is no longer a prison. You can go on a tour of it and see what it was like to live there."

"Can we do that? Please?" Juan and Justin begged Mike and Miss Lake.

"If we can get tickets," Miss Lake said.

"I can see why not many prisoners got off Alcatraz alive," Lisa said. "Look at how rough it is out here!"

They looked down into the dark swirling water beside the island.

"And the water is ice cold," Mike said. "That could finish you off fast."

"The large wooded island you see ahead is Angel Island," the loudspeaker told them. "It was an army base for many years. Now it is a state park. You can hike all over the island."

The wind was blowing the fog around the boat. It was getting harder to see the Golden Gate Bridge ahead.

"We can't even see the city now," Juan said. "It's hidden in the fog."

Suddenly the long loud blast of a foghorn cut through the air. Everybody jumped.

"What was that?" Lisa asked. Her voice sounded scared.

"Just a fog horn on a ship," Mike said. "That's how ships signal each other in fog."

"I don't like this," Lisa said. "We can't see anything around us. There is nothing but fog."

CHAPTER 5

Danger on the Bay

"Ladies and gentlemen, look up and you'll see the Golden Gate Bridge. If you're lucky. The fog has nearly hidden it now," the announcer said. "The bridge was finished in 1937. It is 8,981 feet long, and its towers rise 746 feet above the water."

"I always used to think the bridge was painted gold," Amy said. "But it's really red."

"A lot of people expect that," Mike said.

"This opening in the bay was always called

the Golden Gate even before the bridge was built," Miss Lake explained.

The fog now covered the deck. The wind whipped at the kids' faces. The boat rocked up and down in the dangerous currents under the bridge.

"Mike and I are going down for some hot coffee," Miss Lake told the kids. "You come down too if it gets any rougher up here." They headed down to the snack bar.

Suddenly Juan saw a boy in a wheelchair rolling towards him on the deck. Was he lost from his group? What was he doing all alone out here? The boat rolled sharply and the wheelchair started to tip. Juan grabbed it.

"Whoa there! This is pretty rough up here. Maybe we should get you downstairs," Juan told the younger boy.

"I wanted to see the bridge," the boy said. "You can't see it from down below."

Suddenly the engines stopped. The boat was quiet. It just tossed up and down in the waves. Foghorns blasted in the distance.

"What happened? Why did the engines stop?" Lisa asked.

"Maybe they always turn them off under the bridge," Justin said. "They'll start up again in a minute I bet."

Suddenly the engines started to come on. Then they quickly died.

"Is there something wrong with the boat?" the boy asked Juan.

"No, I'm sure there's not. But if there is, they can fix it. Don't worry. Hey, tell me your name. Mine's Juan."

"It's Ted. Do you think they have lifeboats on board, Juan?"

Juan tried to make his voice sound calm. But he was starting to feel really worried.

"I'm sure they have lifeboats, Ted. But they'll get the boat started again. I know they will," Juan told the boy. But he could see they were drifting close to one of the bridge towers. Were they going to be smashed against it?

CHAPTER 6

Bridge to Safety

"I'd better get you downstairs," Juan told Ted. "They're probably really worried about you. Hey, guys, give me a hand. This deck is slippery."

They all started wheeling the chair towards the ramp. The deck rocked wildly up and down. Juan could see they were drifting closer to the huge tower. His heart was pounding as he pushed the chair. Ted held on tight to Juan's arm.

"Attention!" blared the loudspeaker. "We are having engine trouble. We are taking you off the ship. Please do not be alarmed. The Coast Guard boat is coming up now on the port side. Please go quickly to the lower deck. Do not run. I repeat. Do not run."

So it *was* bad. They had lost the engines. Could they get everyone off before the boat hit the tower?

They started down the ramp with the wheelchair. Two people rushed towards them.

"Ted! You're O.K.! We were so worried!" A man and woman started hugging Ted. Then they turned to Juan and the kids. "You helped him! Thank you!"

Ted would not let go of Juan's arm.

"I'll help him off the boat," Juan told the couple. "You can go get the other kids." The couple rushed off.

People were moving towards a big side door. The kids could see the Coast Guard boat outside. Both boats were tossing up and down. You could hardly stand up. How would they ever get Ted over to the other boat?

"Kids! Here you are! We couldn't find you up on deck. Quickly! Let's get onto the other boat!" Mike told them. "There isn't much time." Then he saw that Juan had Ted to push.

"The chair will never make it across," Mike said. He reached down and picked up

40

Ted. He stepped up to the open door of the boat. Ted had his arms around Mike's neck.

There was a wooden plank across to the other boat. It was about ten feet long. The waves crashed up against it. Sometimes over it. Mike started across with Ted. Miss Lake and the kids watched them go. It was a terrifying sight. Mike made it halfway across. Then two men came out to meet him. They pulled Mike and Ted into the Coast Guard boat. Safe!

Then it was time for the kids to cross.

"Don't look down at the water," Miss Lake told them. "Just keep your eyes on Mike."

The kids started across one at a time.

Mike came out to pull each one into the boat.

Then it was Miss Lake's turn. She was the last of her group to leave the boat. Juan watched her start across. Then he saw the tower. It was right there. The tour boat was about to smash into it.

"Go!" Juan screamed to his teacher.

She must have heard him. She threw herself out towards Mike just as the boat hit the tower. Mike pulled her into the Coast Guard boat. There was a terrible ripping sound as the tour boat broke apart. The last people on board had dived into the water. The Coast Guard men quickly threw ropes to them.

Miss Lake, Mike, and the kids were safe!

But what about the kids in wheelchairs? Were they all O.K. now? The rest of the group went to find out. Juan stayed with Ted.

A loudspeaker came on. "Everyone is now safe. You all did a fine job. You stayed calm. This saved lives. We are leaving for San Francisco now."

Ted looked at Juan and smiled. "It was really neat getting rescued. I thought I'd be scared getting carried over to the Coast Guard boat. But it wasn't so bad."

"Hey, you were pretty brave," Juan said.

Just then Miss Lake, Mike and the kids came around the corner.

"Everybody in Ted's group is fine," Miss

43

Lake said. "Juan, you're really a hero today! I heard how you rescued Ted from up on top."

"No way. This guy was just having problems with that slippery deck," Juan said.

The boat's engines started up.

"What a day! Can you believe it started out with a sunny morning in a cable car house?" Miss Lake said.

"How am I going to get all this on one postcard?" asked Justin.

"And what shall we do tomorrow?" They all laughed together as they looked out the windows and watched San Francisco come closer and closer.